Shall I Knit You a Hat?

A Christmas Yarn

Kate Klise ✳ illustrated by **M. Sarah Klise**

SQUARE FISH

Henry Holt and Company

SQUARE

FISH

An Imprint of Holtzbrinck Publishers

Library of Congress Cataloging-in-Publication Data Available
ISBN-13: 978-0-312-37139-5 / ISBN-10: 0-312-37139-X
Library of Congress Catalog Card Number: 2003022497

Designed by Patrick Collins
The artist used acrylic on Bristol board to create the illustrations for this book.
Originally published in the United States by Henry Holt and Company, LLC
First Square Fish Edition: October 2007
10 9 8 7 6 5 4 3 2 1
www.squarefishbooks.com

"Oh dear. . . . Oh my. . . . Oh goodness me."
These were some of the things Mother Rabbit said

"A blizzard is moving this way," she told Little
Rabbit as she tied his scarf the next morning. "It will
start snowing on Christmas Eve and won't stop until
the snow reaches the tallest tips of your ears."

"My ears?" asked Little Rabbit. "But that will be
very cold."

"You're right," said Mother Rabbit. "Shall I knit you
a hat to keep your ears warm?"

"Yes, please," said Little Rabbit. "A Christmas hat,
just for me."

And so while Little Rabbit was at school, Mother Rabbit knit and purled—*click click clack, click click clack*—to the beat of the music on the radio.

That evening, Mother Rabbit tried the hat on Little
Rabbit. He stood very still while his mother made the
necessary adjustments. "Look how this hat shows off
your long, beautiful ears," said Mother Rabbit.

Little Rabbit agreed. He liked his new hat and wore it even while he ate dinner. During dessert, he thought of something. "What about our friends?" he asked. "Shouldn't we make hats for them, too? We could give them as Christmas presents!"

"Little Rabbit," said his mother, "that idea is so delicious, it deserves a second piece of carrot cake."

The following day, they visited the horse, whose
mane Mother Rabbit measured while Little Rabbit
distracted him by telling a joke.

Next, they visited the goose, whose long neck they inspected without ruffling her feathers.

They found their other friends at the market. Little Rabbit told them a story while Mother Rabbit secretly took measurements.

"That was a little sneaky," Mother Rabbit admitted later that night as she and Little Rabbit ate dinner. "Sneaky, yes," Little Rabbit agreed. "But necessary."

Mother Rabbit let Little Rabbit stay up very late that night—two hours past his bedtime—so he could help

"The cat's hat must be smart and stylish, just like
she is," Little Rabbit said. "The goose's hat will have a
long scarf that wraps around her neck. The horse's hat
should be part blanket so he can sleep in the snow.
And the dog's hat must have an extra-long tail that
looks pretty when it blows in the wind."

"And the deer's hat?" asked Mother Rabbit.

"The deer's hat will show off his lovely antlers."

The next day was Christmas Eve. Late in the afternoon,
Little Rabbit and his mother pulled the gifts into town
on a sled.

When they arrived at the market, all their friends
gathered around to look at the beautifully wrapped gifts.

"Open your presents, please!" said Little Rabbit.
"We made them especially for you."

Little Rabbit held up a mirror. "See how beautiful you look?"

And with that, the wind turned cold and the sky became dark. The first snowflake fell.

"It's time, Little Rabbit," said Mother Rabbit. "We must get back to our house."

"Oh dear. . . . Oh my. . . . Oh goodness me."
These were some of the things the friends said when
the snow began to fall . . . and fall . . . and fall.

"Just look how this clever hat keeps my head warm and dry," said the horse.

"Well, my long neck is perfectly comfortable," said the goose.

"My antlers have never been drier," said the deer.

"Have you noticed how pretty my tail looks when the wind blows?" asked the dog. "It's quite lovely, isn't it?"

Yes, they all agreed. It really was quite lovely.

"If we hurry," said the squirrel, "we can catch up with the Rabbits and thank them..."

...and they did.

"We are lucky," said the cat, "to have such nice friends as you Rabbits."

"Indeed!" chirped the squirrel. "This is the nicest, most thoughtful Christmas present anyone has ever given me."

But then, on the snowy sled ride home, Little
Rabbit had a terrible thought.

"Oh, no!" he said. "Tomorrow is Christmas, and
I forgot to make a present for *you,* Mother."

His mother squeezed him tight.

"Little Rabbit," she said, "being with you is the best gift of all."

Once they were safely home, the Rabbits celebrated
Christmas Eve with a carrot cake, warm from the oven.